The Adventures of SPARROWBOY

The Adventures of

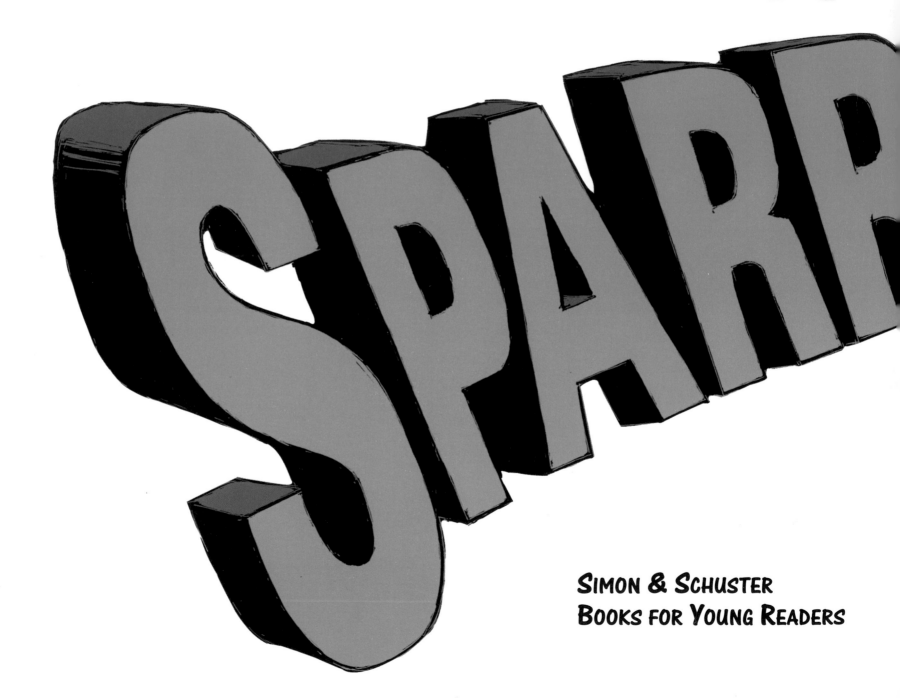

SPARR

SIMON & SCHUSTER
BOOKS FOR YOUNG READERS

OWBOY

BRIAN PINKNEY

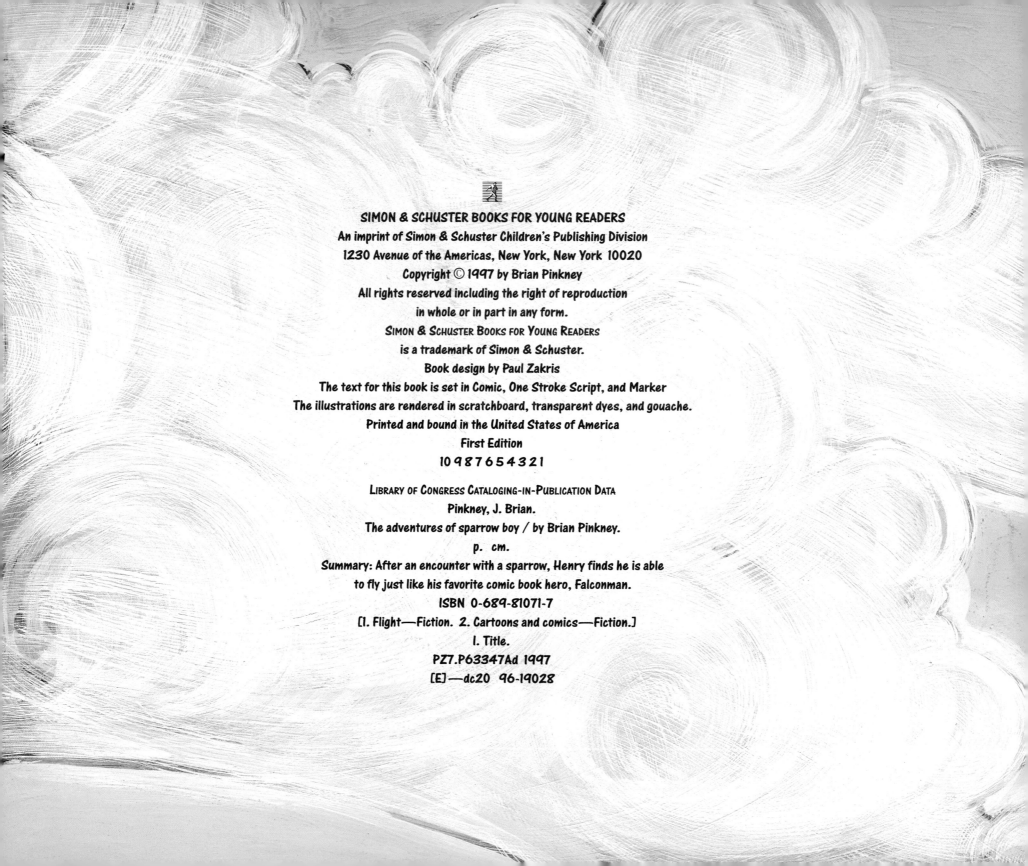

SIMON & SCHUSTER BOOKS FOR YOUNG READERS

An imprint of Simon & Schuster Children's Publishing Division

1230 Avenue of the Americas, New York, New York 10020

SIMON & SCHUSTER BOOKS FOR YOUNG READERS

is a trademark of Simon & Schuster.

Book design by Paul Zakris

The text for this book is set in Comic, One Stroke Script, and Marker

The illustrations are rendered in scratchboard, transparent dyes, and gouache.

Printed and bound in the United States of America

First Edition

10 9 8 7 6 5 4 3 2 1

LIBRARY OF CONGRESS CATALOGING-IN-PUBLICATION DATA

Pinkney, J. Brian.

The adventures of sparrow boy / by Brian Pinkney.

p. cm.

Summary: After an encounter with a sparrow, Henry finds he is able

to fly just like his favorite comic book hero, Falconman.

ISBN 0-689-81071-7

[1. Flight—Fiction. 2. Cartoons and comics—Fiction.]

I. Title.

PZ7.P63347Ad 1997

[E]—dc20 96-19028

Henry the paperboy always read the front page before he started on his route. Then he read the comics.

Sometimes, the headlines got Henry down. "Why does this stuff have to happen?" he asked himself. "If Falconman was here, he'd make things better."

The Adventures of FALCON

BY BARNEY NIPKIN

MAN

It has come to pass that a mystical falcon possesses the gift to transfer his powers to a mortal. That man is Trooper Mark Steed who becomes . . . Falconman, a superhero sworn to defend the defenseless.

ZAP!

WHOOSH!

"Going my way?"

Man and bird return to the transfer site.

ZAP!

To be continued...

Later, as Henry rode along Thurber Street
tossing papers onto porches, a sparrow swooped
down and landed in the middle of his path.
    "Hey! Get out of my way!" Henry jammed on
the brakes and . . .

Henry flew over the handlebars and soared to the sky.

LOOP-DE-LOOP!

"I can fly!" Henry shouted.

OH NO! HERE COMES TROUBLE . . .

GRRRR!

Bruno the bully marched up Thurber Street with Wolf. Then Bruno let Wolf go.

HE'S HUNTING THE TWO RASCALS!
WOOF!
RRRRR!!!!
Will and Matt had been bitten once too often.

IN THE NICK OF TIME . . .

"Sit, doggie!"

"You were almost a sparrow sandwich," Henry said.

MEANWHILE . . . BRUNO WAS STILL UP TO NO GOOD.

"Hey, Dawn! Does your cat have nine lives?"

"Hey, Bruno! Do you???"

WHAT'S THIS? DOUBLE TROUBLE!

"Let's catch that little birdie . . .

. . . and keep him in our laboratory."

"Now you see him, now you don't!" said Henry.

"You'll be out of danger there," Henry said, "and I can finish delivering my papers."

"I don't get it. Why can't you fly?"

THERE'S JUST ONE WAY TO FIND OUT!

Together, Henry and the sparrow returned

to the place where they had first collided.

All was quiet along Thurber
Street as Henry rode home. Trouble
was nowhere to be seen.

And everything felt just a little better.